Poems for Mothers

POEMS FOR MOTHERS

selected by

Myra Cohn Livingston

illustrated by

Deborah Kogan Ray

HOLIDAY HOUSE / NEW YORK

Another one for Mother
M.C.L.

To my mother
D.K.R.

Text copyright © 1988 by Myra Cohn Livingston
Illustrations copyright © 1988 by Deborah Kogan
All rights reserved
Printed in the United States of America
First Edition

Library of Congress Cataloging-in-Publication Data

Poems for mothers.

Summary: A collection of poems by a variety of
authors about mothers.
1. Children's poetry, American.   2. Mother and
child—Juvenile poetry.   3. American poetry—
20th century.   [1. Mother and child—Poetry.
2. American poetry—Collections]   I. Livingston,
Myra Cohn.   II. Ray, Deborah, ill.   III. Title.
PS595.M64P64   1988   811'.5'0803520431   87–19629
ISBN 0–8234–0678–4

CONTENTS

My Mother's Face

I see my mother's face at the door,
I see her waiting inside the warm car.
Alone and waiting; her breath clouds the window.

I feel her hand on my face in the dark
when the dark opens up for her like a flower.
I feel my mother's cool hand on my cheek,
the pretty, loose skin on the back of her wrist.

I hear my mother's voice in the kitchen,
murmuring, rising, or shrieking in anger.
Listen! She's humming a little tune.

Days and nights—
long, busy days or
sad, slow nights.
My mother opens the door to my room.
I see my mother's face at the door.

LIZ ROSENBERG

I Hear My Mother's

soft voice reading
poems to me
words like music
over and over

I hear the sound
of her cooking spoon
beating against a white bowl
in her sweet-smelling kitchen

I hear her car
turning into
the driveway
home from work

I hear her heels taptapping
as she comes
into the bedroom
to kiss me good-night

and I feel
her smooth skin
as she takes me in her arms
and holds me tight

RUTH WHITMAN

7

Mama's Song

Mama hums a sea-song with her eyes;
a deep blue rising sea-song,
moving as her eyes move,
weaving foam across my face.

White gulls whirl overhead;
the sun washes back and forth,
and I am rocking . . .
rocking . . .
      like a boat
in the waves
      of her song.

DEBORAH CHANDRA

9

Don't Be Afraid

Don't be afraid, my child, those are
only two mice, jumping down from the
table to the chair. They are smaller
than you and couldn't gobble you up.

Don't be afraid, my child, that's only
the rain's finger tapping wetly on the
window. We won't let it in.

Hide deep inside me, I am your mother.
We'll pull the dark night over our
heads and no one will find us.

DAVID VOGEL
translated by T. Carmi

10

House Noises

My mother's big on little fears.
When darkness falls, she sharpens ears:

Outside—who gave that awful shriek?
The storm door that the wind makes creak.

Now what was that? That scraping sound?
Only a leaf blown over ground.

What scurried in the attic? Mice?
The sliding-off-the-roof of ice.

At the back door—did someone cough?
No, but our drainpipe just dropped off.

X. J. KENNEDY

My Natural Mama

my natural mama
is gingerbread
all brown and
spicy sweet.
some mamas are rye
or white or
golden wheat
but my natural mama
is gingerbread,
brown and spicy sweet.

LUCILLE CLIFTON

12

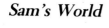

Sam's World

sam's mother has
grey combed hair

she will never touch
it with a hot iron

she leaves it
the way the lord
intended

she wears it proudly
a black and grey
round head of hair

SAM CORNISH

13

Working with Mother

Some of the time
I get on the bus
with mother

(just the two of us)

and we go to the place
where she works all day.

We take some games
so I can play,

and some of the time
I help a lot
with work that mother

just forgot——
(or couldn't finish—
or did all wrong——)

It's good
she needs me
to come along.

MYRA COHN LIVINGSTON

15

My Mother

My mother
Wasn't like
Some others.

She didn't
Make cakes or
Candied apples;

She sat down
Beside her
Sewing basket

And stayed
Up late
Reading poetry.

VALERIE WORTH

New Mother

She came to take
my mother's
place.

I like her smile.

I like her face.

I like the way
        she talks to me
        although it's seldom
        we agree
                on bedtime
                or some places where
                I go.

                        But then
        she seems to care.

        And often, when
        we both get mad
        and have to settle things
        with Dad

at least
we learn about each other.

I'm sort of getting used to—
Mother.

R. H. MARKS

I See a Star

I see a star
      yet it is day.
The hands of my mother
      make it grow.
It is a black star
      set against a white sky.

How gentle that star.
Now that she weaves
devils' claws
Together to make
      a basket.

ALONZO LOPEZ

Mom Is Wow!

Mothers are finders and keepers
They are comforters of weepers
They are lullers-abye for sleepers.

Mothers are good-manners makers
They are temperature takers
They are the best of birthday bakers.
            Mom is Wow!

Mothers are sick-bed sit besiders
They are hiding place providers
They are pin-the-tail guiders.

Mothers are prayer makers in the nights
They are enders of quarrels and fights
They are teachers of duties and rights.
            Mom is Wow!

JULIA FIELDS

20

When Mom Plays Just for Me

My mom is playing piano with Sidney.
I like making my bed to the music
that bubbles under my bedroom door.

Mom and Sidney are still playing piano.
I like pouring milk over my cornflakes
trying to match the tinklings that spill into the kitchen.

Now Sidney's gone home. Mom plays just for me
and I run around in circles in the living room
and collapse on the lambskin under the piano.

I look up. I see the hardwood and pedals
of the moving hammers and strings—
the piano's heart—when Mom plays just for me.

APRIL HALPRIN WAYLAND

21

Pippin in the Evening

Mommy,
Mommy,
tell me
why
I'm the
apple
of your
eye?

Why not
cherry,
why not
plum,
why not
lingon-
berry
Mom?

And what
sort of
apple—
sweet,
like a
tickle
in your
feet?

22

Yes, what
sort of
apple—
tart,
like a
wild thing
in your
heart?

Green as
green gage,
red as
blush;
Grannie
Smith,
or
McIntosh?

If you
love me
tell me
I
am the
pippin
of your
eye.

When you
kiss me
tell me,
do,
that I'm
yummy
through and
through.

N. M. BODECKER

One, Two, Three, Four M-O-T-H-E-R

One: I do not like the way
         that she can glare at me.

Two: I do not like her being
         nearly everywhere with me.

Three: I do not like some things
         she sometimes makes me eat.

And   I do not like at all
  Four   her *taking* me across the street.

BUT!

One: I like the things she plans
         that both of us can play.

Two: I like her listening
         to stuff I have to say.

Three: I like the way the two
         of us can sing.

And   It's just I *like* her
  Four   in spite of everything.

FELICE HOLMAN

24

Free Time

Light comes back again and I
take my tattered bear and creep
mouse-quiet downstairs.

A little click—the TV's on
and we stay warm under a robe,
watch Sylvester, Bugs, and friends.

Pretty soon Mommy comes by, says "Hi,"
gives us a kiss, a glass of juice.
But Teddy's never thirsty!

JIM THOMAS

Chore Boy

Too young to milk
our cows, throw corn
to pigs or chickens,

I make my bed,
pile dirty clothes
in tall hampers.

I fill a brown sack
from wastebaskets,
am careful with matches.

I watch dancing
flames' bright orange,
a smoking barrel.

But best—Mom says,
"Clean this for me!"
Chocolate icing pan!

JIM THOMAS

27

Gift

This is mint and here are three pinks
I have brought you, Mother.
They are wet with rain
And shining with it.
The pinks smell like more of them
In a blue vase:
The mint smells like summer
In many gardens.

HILDA CONKLING

My Mother and I

My mother and I
rip two rosebuds
from the rosebush in our yard,
and we slip a bit of branch
into each rosebud
and make ourselves pipes.
Then we puff on them
and laugh and laugh.

EMANUEL DI PASQUALE

Sugarfields

treetalk and windsong are
the language of my mother
her music does not leave me.

let me taste again the cane
the syrup of the earth
sugarfields were once my home.

i would lie down in the fields
and never get up again
(treetalk and windsong
are the language of my mother
sugarfields are my home)

the leaves go on whispering secrets
as the wind blows a tune in the grass
my mother's voice is in the fields
this music cannot leave me.

BARBARA MAHONE

ACKNOWLEDGMENTS

Grateful acknowledgment is also made for the following reprints:

Acum Ltd. for the original (Hebrew) version by the author and Penguin Books Ltd. for "Don't Be Afraid" by David Vogel from *The Penguin Book of Hebrew Verse* edited and translation by T. Carmi (Allen Lane/Penguin Books, 1981), translation copyright © T. Carmi, 1981. Reprinted by permission of Acum Ltd. and Penguin Books Ltd.

Atheneum Publishers, Inc. for "House Noises" from *The Forgetful Wishing Well* by X. J. Kennedy. Copyright © 1985 by X. J. Kennedy. (A Margaret K. McElderry Book). Reprinted with the permission of Atheneum Publishers, Inc.

Hilda Conkling for "Gift" from *Poems by a Little Girl*. Frederick A. Stokes, 1920. Copyright Hilda Conkling 1920, 1921, and 1949.

Doubleday for "I See a Star" by Alonzo Lopez from *The Whispering Wind* edited by Terry Allen. Copyright © 1972 by the Institute of American Indian Arts. Reprinted by permission of Doubleday & Company, Inc.

Farrar, Straus & Giroux, Inc. for "Sam's World" by Sam Cornish from *Natural Process: An Anthology of New Black Poetry* edited by Ted Wilentz and Tom Weatherly. Copyright © 1970 by Hill and Wang. Reprinted by permission of Hill and Wang, a division of Farrar, Straus and Giroux, Inc.

Barbara Mahone for "Sugarfields" from *Sugarfields*, published by Broadside Press, 1970.

Ruth Whitman for "I Hear My Mother's." Copyright © 1988 by Ruth Whitman.

Valerie Worth for "My Mother." Copyright © 1988 by Valerie Worth Bahlke.

Grateful acknowledgment is made to the following poets, whose work was especially commissioned for this book:

N. M. Bodecker for "Pippin in the Evening." Copyright © 1988 by N. M. Bodecker.

Deborah Chandra for "Mama's Song." Copyright © 1988 by Deborah Chandra.

Lucille Clifton for "My Natural Mama." Copyright © 1988 by Lucille Clifton.

Emanuel di Pasquale for "My Mother and I." Copyright © 1988 by Emanuel di Pasquale.

Julia Fields for "Mom Is Wow!" Copyright © 1988 by Julia Fields.

Felice Holman for "One, Two, Three, Four M-O-T-H-E-R." Copyright © 1988 by Felice Holman.

Myra Cohn Livingston for "Working with Mother." Copyright © 1988 by Myra Cohn Livingston.

R. H. Marks for "New Mother." Copyright © 1988 by R. H. Marks.

Liz Rosenberg for "My Mother's Face." Copyright © 1988 by Liz Rosenberg.

Jim Thomas for "Chore Boy" and "Free Time." Copyright © 1988 by Jim Thomas.

April Halprin Wayland for "When Mom Plays Just for Me." Copyright © 1988 by April Halprin Wayland.